## – Chapter 1: Epic Warriors –

Mark Gannon had a smile on his face as he walked down the street with his friend Alex. Mark held an unopened pack of Epic Warriors cards in his hands. He rubbed the cellophane wrapper.

Mark and Alex had just left the local comics and gaming shop. While there, they'd each bought a new deck of playing cards. Alex had already opened his. He flipped through his new cards as they walked.

"Score," Alex said, grinning. He held a card up in Mark's face. "This armor card is going to boost my Warrior's defense to the max," he boasted. "AngerHeart will be unbeatable now."

AngerHeart was the Warrior Card Alex always played. He was the best warrior that Alex or Mark knew of. Mark was tired of getting smashed whenever they played.

Mark tapped the unopened deck in his hand. "We'll see about that," he said.

"Then let's see what you got this time!" Alex said, pointing at Mark's deck.

"I never open mine until we get home," Mark said. "You know that."

Alex shook his head and grinned. "Whatever, man," he said. "Doesn't matter — you're not going to get a new Warrior Card good enough to beat AngerHeart."

# JASON STRANGE

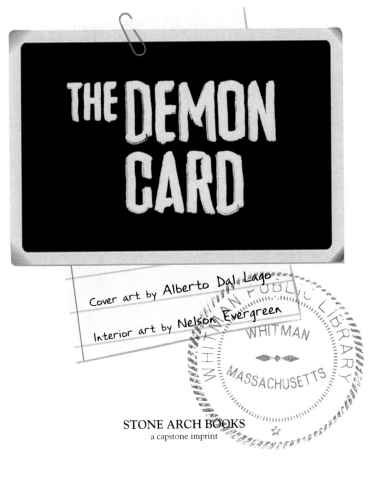

## THE DEMON CARD

Cover art by Alberto Dal Lago

Interior art by Nelson Evergreen

STONE ARCH BOOKS
a capstone imprint

Jason Strange is published by Stone Arch Books
A Capstone Imprint
1710 Roe Crest Dr.
North Mankato, Minnesota 56003
www.capstonepub.com

Copyright © 2012 by Stone Arch Books

Cataloging-in-Publication Data is available at the Library of Congress website.

ISBN: 978-1-4342-3296-0 (library binding)
ISBN: 978-1-4342-3884-9 (paperback)

Summary: Whenever Mark puts his new, ultra-rare trading card into play, bad things
happen to his opponents — *after* the game has ended . . .

Art Director: Kay Fraser
Graphic Designer: Hilary Wacholz
Production Specialist: Michelle Biedscheid

Photo credits:
Shutterstock: Nikita Rogul (handcuffs, p. 2); Stephen Mulcahey (police badge, p. 2);
B&T Media Group (blank badge, p. 2); Picsfive (coffee stain, pp. 2, 5, 12, 17, 24, 30,
42, 48, 57); Andy Dean Photography (paper, pen, coffee, pp. 2, 66); osov (blank notes,
p. 1); Thomas M Perkins (folder with blank paper, pp. 66, 67); M.E. Mulder (black
electrical tape, pp. 69, 70, 71)

Printed and bound in the USA.

011917   010241R

# TABLE OF CONTENTS

Alex's apartment was just ahead. He lived above Ravens Pass Grocery on Main Street. When they reached the door, Mark and Alex sprinted up the three flights of stairs, into the apartment, and to Alex's bedroom. As soon as they were inside, Mark tore open his new pack of cards.

Slowly and carefully, Mark flipped over his first card to reveal an armored shield. "Garbage," Alex announced.

Mark's next card was a pair of leather gloves. "Hmph," Alex grunted. "Useless." Mark rolled his eyes.

Mark lifted another card to reveal a wooden battle-axe. Alex shook his head. "My hero's war mace is ten times better than that weapon," he bragged. He jabbed Mark with his elbow. "This is a terrible deck — so much for good luck, huh?"

Mark sighed. He flipped several more cards, with Alex ridiculing each card after each flip. When there was only one more card left, Mark turned it over very slowly.

Mark's eyes went wide. "What — what is this?" he whispered. The card looked different from the others. Its edges were adorned with gold, making the borders dance with light. Along the top, the words that Mark had been hoping to see were written in silver letters: Epic Warrior!

This one's name was DeathBringer, and he was no ordinary Warrior. The monstrous figure stood in a blazing inferno, swinging a wicked morning star over his head. Dark steel armor — the strongest armor type in the entire game — covered his body. Red, burning eyes seemed to be smoldering right through the card itself.

And the best thing? DeathBringer wielded a Skull Shield that doubled his Armor Class.

"I guess it's a new Epic Warrior," Alex said. "But look at that." He pointed at the bottom of the card, where the hero's faction was written: Demon.

"I've never heard of a demon faction," Mark said. "AngerHeart is human, and my other warrior, GraceBlood, is an elf. But a demon? There's no such thing."

Alex shrugged. "How are his stats?" he asked.

Mark flipped the card over and read through DeathBringer's stats and special abilities. "Wow," he said. "His Armor Class is twice as high as AngerHeart's."

"What?" Alex said. He snatched the metallic card and looked for himself. "Thirty-nine AC?!" Alex cried.

"Yup," Mark said. He nodded. "And look at his special abilities."

Alex read, "Cascade of Fire. Armor Decay. Coma Blow. Presence." Then he handed the card back to Mark. Mark took it, smiling, and gazed at the demon figure on the front.

"AngerHeart has the Presence ability too," Alex said. "I don't even know what Presence does."

Mark shrugged. "Me either," he said. "Probably has something to do with an expansion pack. That would also explain why DeathBringer is the only demon I've ever seen. Maybe the new expansion will come out next year?"

"Maybe," Alex said. "Either way, you're going to be unbeatable with that Warrior — even without using his special abilities."

Mark's smile got even bigger.

"I'm going to challenge Greg tomorrow," Mark said.

There was a knock on the door. Alex's mom called out, "Mark, your father's on the phone. You're late for dinner."

Mark pulled his phone from his pocket. The battery was dead. "Oops," he said. "I'd better get home."

"Hold on a sec," Alex said. He sat at his desk and turned on his computer. "Let's check the forums to see if anyone's heard of this card or a demon faction."

Mark sat on the edge of the bed and handed Alex the card. "All right," he said, glancing at the clock. "But make it fast."

"I will, I will," Alex said. He quickly scanned the card, and then posted the image to a discussion board about the game.

In the subject line, Alex wrote the word "DeathBringer." In the post itself, he attached the image of the card and wrote, "Does anyone have this card? Since when is there a demon faction?"

Alex handed the card back to Mark. "There you go," he said. "Hopefully someone will reply."

Mark scooped up the rest of his deck and grabbed his bag. "Okay, tell me tomorrow," he said. "I'll see you at school."

"See ya," Alex called out. As he turned back to his computer, he saw that a reply had already popped up on the forum. In bold, red letters, it read, "THAT CARD MUST BE DESTROYED."

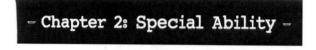

## – Chapter 2: Special Ability –

Early the next morning, Mark and Alex met on their walk to Ravens Pass Middle School. Alex filled Mark in on the forum post. "That's it?" Mark asked. "He just said to destroy the card?"

"Nope," Alex said, chuckling. "His second message said we should send it to him because he has to recite a certain spell while burning the card."

"Yeah, right," Mark said. "He just wants the card for himself."

"Agreed," Alex said. "It must be pretty valuable."

"Must be," Mark said. "So, nobody said anything about the demon faction?"

Alex shook his head. "Nothing worth repeating," he said. "A few people said we made it up, that it was fake, stuff like that."

Mark pulled open the double doors to their school. "Figures," he said. "See you at lunch."

"Later," Alex said.

* * *

The school day went by slowly. Mark couldn't keep his eyes off the clock. He was counting down the minutes until lunch, because he was planning to challenge Greg at Epic Warriors.

Greg had the best deck in school, and he always knew what card to play. He had never lost a single match.

When lunch finally came, Mark sat down at the corner circular table in the cafeteria. Greg was already there. His coat was over the chair next to him. He had a big smirk on his face as he shuffled his deck.

"So," Greg said as Mark took out his own deck, "you looking to get embarrassed by me again, Mark?"

Mark glanced at Alex and returned his smirk. He pulled out DeathBringer and slid the card across the table to Greg.

Greg scooped it up smoothly. He whistled. "DeathBringer, huh?" he said. "Nice stats."

He read the abilities out loud. "Demon Dagger: 'Plus 100 attack power against demons,'" he said.

"That's kinda useless until there are some other demon cards in the game," Greg said.

Mark smirked. "Just check out the other special abilities," he said.

Greg glanced at DeathBringer's other attacks. "Four special abilities?" he said. "Most only have one or two. That should come in pretty handy."

Greg handed the card back to Mark. "Then again, if you can't get through my warriors," Greg said, "none of that will do you much good."

"We'll see," Mark said. "You ready?"

"Always," Greg replied. He passed his deck to Mark, and Mark shuffled it. Then Greg shuffled Mark's deck. The battle began.

Mark's first few attacks did no damage. Whatever he tried, Greg's warriors blocked.

"Thought so," Greg said. "I'll wear down your warrior eventually."

Almost all of Greg's attacks were landing, since most of Mark's equipment cards weren't very good. Then Mark came up with an idea. He decided to use one of DeathBringer's special abilities. He said, "I cast Armor Decay." Then he turned his warrior card to show that one of the warrior's abilities was being used.

Greg had to remove all his equipment cards from the game. Now only his warriors and their allies could protect him.

"Now you're in trouble," Alex said from over Mark's shoulder. "Mark will definitely land his next —"

"Actually," said a voice above them, "now you're *all* in trouble."

It was Mr. Snyder, their gym teacher. "You boys have been told you're not allowed to play this game in school," he said. "Now put the cards away before I take them."

Greg nodded and smiled. "Yes sir, Mr. Snyder," he said. He scooped up his cards and put them back in his deck case.

Mr. Snyder grunted and walked away. "You're lucky," Mark said to Greg. "If Mr. Snyder hadn't ended that battle, I would've beaten you."

Greg shrugged as he got up from the table. "Not likely," he said. "But Armor Decay is a great ability. I'll be sure to wait until the next expansion before I face you again."

"Chicken," Alex said.

Greg chuckled and walked away.

As Greg passed the lunch line, three big guys wearing letter jackets bumped into him. Greg stumbled into the garbage bins against the wall. His books and his bag fell to the ground, spilling papers and books everywhere. Even worse, Greg's deck case slammed into the tiled wall. The case sprang open on impact, sending his cards flying into the garbage bin.

The guys in the letter jackets laughed as Greg jumped to his feet and ran to the bin. As Greg lifted a handful of cards from the garbage, Mark saw that the cards were covered in tomato sauce and warm milk.

The cards were ruined — every single one of them.

## — Chapter 3: Just a Card —

After school, Alex and Mark walked along Main Street toward Alex's apartment. "That was hilarious!" Alex said. "Poor Greg, he'll need to spend a fortune to rebuild his deck now."

Mark was staring at his DeathBringer card as they walked. "You don't think it's a little weird?" Mark asked. "I mean, I cast Armor Decay — an equipment-destroying spell. Then, seconds later, all of Greg's cards were ruined by those bullies!"

"Yeah," Alex said, chuckling. "Pretty funny coincidence."

"I don't know if it was just a coincidence," Mark said softly.

Alex rolled his eyes. "Oh, give me a break," he said. "Next you're gonna tell me that you believe in magic."

Alex's constant teasing was starting to get on Mark's nerves. He pulled out his deck of cards and tossed his bag onto the bench at a bus stop. "Let's play," Mark said.

"Right here?" Alex said, pointing at the bus bench.

Mark grinned. "Why not?" he asked. "You scared?"

Alex sighed. "Fine," he said. He took out his own cards. "But this is really silly."

Alex's hero, AngerHeart, did not have the stellar equipment Greg had. But AngerHeart attacked faster, and every three turns he got a free bonus attack. This meant the best way to beat him was to slow him down.

Mark looked at DeathBringer's special abilities. If he used Coma Blow, AngerHeart would be powerless for three turns. It would give DeathBringer a chance to land a couple of big attacks before Alex could counter.

Mark looked into Alex's eyes and said, "Coma Blow." He tapped the card.

Alex frowned. Now he couldn't call upon his allies or attack. AngerHeart was a sitting duck.

Over the next three turns, Mark landed three powerful attacks. By the time AngerHeart came out of his coma, he had lost nearly all of his health points.

Two turns later, AngerHeart died. "Well, you won," Alex said, packing up his cards. "But nothing bad happened to me. AngerHeart was in a coma for three rounds, and I'm not in a coma." Alex chuckled. "So I still get the last laugh, dork."

"Yeah, yeah," Mark said, feeling kind of foolish. "So I got a little carried away."

"You think?" Alex said, smirking. He stood up from the bus stop bench. "Anyway, I gotta head home."

"See you later," Mark said.

Alex stepped off the curb to cross the street. He didn't see the bus pulling in to the bus stop. It hit him, and Alex flew across the pavement. He landed in the intersection with a sickening thud.

Mark screamed.

## Chapter 4: Cascade of Fire

The next morning, Mark sat next to Alex's parents in the hospital. They were all waiting to hear how Alex was doing. Mark had been at the hospital all night, ever since Alex had been hit by the bus.

The bus had been about to stop, so it hadn't been going very fast. Still, Alex had been knocked out and hadn't woken up during the ambulance ride.

Mark looked up to see a doctor walking toward them.

"Alex has a broken rib and possibly a concussion," the doctor said. "He's asleep now, but he should wake up soon."

Alex's parents sighed with relief. Mark cleared his throat. "Can I see him?" he asked the doctor. Then he glanced at Alex's parents. They nodded.

The doctor put a hand on Mark's shoulder. "Go ahead," he said. "But please be quiet."

"Okay," Mark said. He slowly walked down the hall toward Alex's room.

As he gently opened the door, he saw that Alex was lying in his hospital bed with his eyes closed. A couple of machines were hooked up to him. He had bandages on his head and one hand, and his ribs were covered in white gauze.

Mark sat down in a chair next to the bed. *Oh, man,* he thought. *Alex is in bad shape.*

He took out his DeathBringer card and flipped it over in his hands. "I knew it," Mark whispered. "I knew this card was cursed."

"Dork," a voice said. Mark lifted his head and smiled. Alex was staring and smirking at him.

Mark leaned forward. "You're awake?!" he said.

Alex nodded slowly. He let out a raspy chuckle.

"So, do you believe me now?" Mark asked.

Alex shrugged and shook his head. "Coincidence," he said hoarsely.

Mark frowned. He took out his deck and began to set up a game on the table next to the bed.

Mark placed DeathBringer across from his other Warrior card, GraceBlood.

"What are you doing?" Alex asked.

"I'm going to prove that this card is cursed by playing against myself," Mark said. He tapped GraceBlood. "And no one is in any danger this time — except me."

Alex narrowed his eyes. "Stop," he said. He started to sit up, but he let out a groan and cradled his ribs with his hands.

"I'm playing DeathBringer's special ability now," Mark said. "Cascade of Fire."

Alex sat up a little. "Well?" he asked. "Did it kill your other warrior?"

"GraceBlood is down to . . . ten health points," Mark said.

"Then finish her off," Alex said.

Mark nodded. He attacked once more with DeathBringer, killing GraceBlood. "Done," Mark said.

The two boys sat in silence. A few moments later, Alex spoke up. "See?" he said. "Nothing bad happened to you." He grinned. "You're just a dork."

Mark packed up his cards. "Maybe," he said uncertainly. "Anyway, I'm going to get the doctor and tell him you're awake."

Alex nodded and laid back onto his bed. As Mark opened the door, an orderly zipped past him with a cart of oxygen tanks. The room door scraped against the metal cart and created a tiny spark. It was just enough to light the leaking oxygen from one of the tanks. A wide plume of fire blasted out from the tanks, sending Mark flying back into Alex's room.

The door slammed closed, trapping the fire in the hall. Alarms began to sound and the sprinkler system clicked on. The fire continued to rage outside the room. Inside, Mark climbed to his feet. His hair and clothes were singed, but he wasn't injured.

"Now do you believe it?" Mark said between coughs.

Alex's eyes were wide. "What should we do?" he asked nervously.

Mark gently removed the IV from his friend's arm. "We have to get out of here," he said. "Let's get you dressed."

Mark helped Alex climb out of bed. He pulled on his jeans and sweatshirt over his hospital gown.

"Think you can handle climbing out?" Mark asked.

Alex cradled his ribs with his left arm and walked to the window. With his other hand, Alex grabbed the latch on the window and threw it open. He looked over his shoulder at Mark with a determined look on his face. "Let's go," he said.

\* \* \*

Moments later, Alex and Mark reached the other side of the huge hospital parking lot. Alex sat down carefully on the grass. He was out of breath and wheezing. "I need to stop," he said.

Mark looked back at the hospital. Smoke was coming from a few windows on the first floor, but it didn't look too bad. A fire truck's siren wailed in the distance, getting closer by the second.

Mark sat down next to Alex. "Told you that card is cursed," Mark said.

Alex nodded. "I guess so," he said. He lay back on the grass. Then he dug into his jeans pocket. "The warning!" he said. He pulled out his phone.

"What warning?" Mark asked.

"We have to find the person who posted on that forum," Alex said. He fumbled with the phone, but dropped it. He grabbed his ribs and grunted.

Alex picked his phone up and tapped the screen. Through gritted teeth, he said, "We have to destroy the card."

Mark grabbed his friend's phone. "Let me," Mark said. He opened the discussion board and found the post. Then he quickly emailed the person who'd left the message.

Mark's face scrunched up and his eyes narrowed. "That's weird," he said.

"What's weird?" Alex asked.

Mark held up the phone so Alex could see it. The poster's name was AngerHeart.

Alex coughed. "So?" he said impatiently.

Mark pulled out DeathBringer and turned the card over in his hands. "You don't think . . ." Mark said, trailing off.

Alex looked at him. "Think what?" he said.

"AngerHeart," Mark said. "Do you think it was the real AngerHeart that warned us?"

Alex chuckled. "There are probably a thousand guys with the same username," he said. "There is no real AngerHeart, dork. It's just a playing card."

Mark held up a playing card to Alex's face. "Just like there's no real DeathBringer?" he asked.

Alex snatched the card. "We don't know he's real," he said. "We only know the card is . . . cursed. Or something."

"Oh, he's real," Mark said. He took the card back and stared at the demonic image on the front.

"Whatever," Alex said. "Just destroy it. Rip it in half — *now*."

Mark grabbed the card with both his hands. He flexed his arms and twisted as hard as he could. The card stayed straight. "It's made of a weird metal, or something," Mark said. "I can't even bend it."

Alex's phone chirped. He clicked through to see a new message. "It's from AngerHeart," he said. "It just says, 'Put me in play, and cast 'Presence'."

"The special ability?" Mark asked. "But it isn't even in the game yet."

Alex dug through his bag and found his AngerHeart card. "Set up a battle," he said.

"Fine," Mark said. Without shuffling or giving it much thought, he laid out cards for a battle between the two warriors. "Do it."

"I cast Presence," Alex said, tapping AngerHeart's card.

Thunder clapped. Mark and Alex jerked their heads up just as a bolt of lightning streaked down from the sky and struck the earth in front of the boys.

The blast of blinding white light was so bright that Mark and Alex had to cover their eyes. When Mark pulled his hand away and squinted, he saw a gigantic man standing before him.

"You have summoned AngerHeart!" the warrior roared.

## Chapter 5: AngerHeart

AngerHeart stomped toward the boys, his steel boots shaking the earth. "You should have heeded my warning and destroyed that card!" the warrior shouted. "Give it to me."

Mark glanced at Alex, then stood up. With a trembling hand, he held out his DeathBringer card. AngerHeart snatched it away. Mark was amazed at how quickly the warrior moved his heavily armored hands.

AngerHeart held the card before his face.

"You foolish boys," the warrior said. "You have interfered with powers beyond your understanding."

"We — we didn't know," Alex said. "It's just a game!"

"A game?" AngerHeart roared. "A game is something little children play while their mommies look on. Are you little children?"

Mark and Alex just stared at the warrior. Neither spoke.

"This," AngerHeart said, gripping the metallic card between two gloved fingers, "is the fiercest of all Warriors. To the demon race, DeathBringer is a god. He should have remained imprisoned inside this card . . . but you two fools have released him into this world!"

"We didn't mean to!" Mark protested.

AngerHeart sighed. "It matters not," he said. He put a hand on Mark's shoulder. The boy felt the warrior looking at him sternly. "Our course is clear. We must finally destroy DeathBringer."

"Okay," Alex said. "You have the card. Do your thing."

AngerHeart shook his head. "It is not that simple," he said. "Had you listened to my warning at once, I could have destroyed the demon with the card. Now he is too powerful, thanks to this game of yours."

"So, what do we do?" Mark asked.

AngerHeart looked around. They were on the edge of the hospital parking lot. Two fire trucks had pulled up to the hospital and the fire fighters were just heading inside.

Since the alarm bells were still ringing, everyone in the hospital was being escorted out. The parking lot was beginning to fill up with doctors, nurses, patients, and families.

"This place is too crowded," the warrior said. "It is not suitable for battle."

"Where should we go?" Alex asked.

"A big, open space," AngerHeart said. "There should be no other people around. Just me and the demon — and you two meddlers, of course. Take me to your grandest arena!"

Mark smirked. "I know just the place," he said. "Follow me."

## Chapter 6: The Demon Card

Mark led the warrior and Alex to the Ravens Pass High School football stadium. It was still early on Saturday morning, so no one was around. The two boys and their armor-clad companion stood on the fifty-yard line.

"This battleground will be adequate," AngerHeart said.

"Is this really necessary?" Alex asked. "I mean, can't you just use your axe to cut the card to pieces?"

"Destroying the card while the demon lives," AngerHeart replied, "would free him into your world. He would take over your nations and rule over all humans."

AngerHeart leaned toward Mark, inches from his face. "Is that what you want?" he growled. His hot breath hit Mark's face like a punch.

"No," Mark said quickly.

"Exactly," AngerHeart said. "So I must defeat him in battle. Only then will we bring an end to his evil for good."

The warrior pulled the axe from its sheath on his back. He lifted his shield and held it across his chest. He was ready to fight.

"Summon the demon!" AngerHeart shouted. "Call forth DeathBringer!"

Mark blinked. Alex cleared his throat. The boys stared blankly at each other.

AngerHeart lowered his shield a few inches. "What are you waiting for, boy?" AngerHeart said. "Release the demon. I am ready."

"Um," Mark said, "how?"

AngerHeart sighed loudly. "How did you summon me?" he asked in an annoyed voice.

"I cast your special ability, Presence," Alex said.

AngerHeart got into his battle stance again. "Then do it again," he growled.

Mark quickly set up his decks. He placed his hand on his DeathBringer card and paused. He glanced up at AngerHeart. "Are you sure about this?" he asked. AngerHeart nodded.

As Mark tapped the card, he braced himself for the worst. "I cast 'Presence'," he said.

Immediately, heavy black clouds began to roll across the horizon. Lightning rippled across AngerHeart's silver armor.

Thunder boomed so loudly that Alex and Mark fell to their knees and covered their ears.

A great crimson flame blasted upward from the center of the field. Alex and Mark shielded their faces, but couldn't look away. As soon the flame died down, smoke that stank of sulfur and death settled on the grass. As it began to fade, they saw the shadow of a figure emerge.

On the scorched grass stood DeathBringer. His image on the card had been impressive — even a little creepy, if Mark was completely honest. But in person, DeathBringer was bigger than Mark had expected. He towered over even AngerHeart, making the gigantic knight look small.

The great demon threw down his weapon and shield. Then he let loose a violent roar.

Suddenly, his hands burst into flames. He brought his flaming, armor-covered, fists upward slowly, as if he were lifting an object off the ground. A ring of fire surrounded the stadium's field, trapping them all inside the flames.

"Now," DeathBringer's voice boomed out. "Who has challenged me?!"

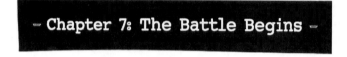

## Chapter 7: The Battle Begins

"I will need your help," AngerHeart cried out to Mark. "Play all your cards. Help me in any way you can!"

With that, the great warrior raised his battle-axe over his head and charged at the demon. DeathBringer turned to face him, lifting his shield tight to his armored face.

Mark and Alex scrambled to get their decks set up. They flipped through their cards, looking for any that would help a human warrior like AngerHeart.

Mark laid out a few ally cards, then looked up at the fight. AngerHeart was behind his shield, blocking blast after blast from DeathBringer's fiery mace. With each strike, AngerHeart's shield cracked more and more until it shattered, sending AngerHeart to his knees.

"We need a healer!" Alex shouted.

Mark nodded and played a healer card. When he did, the human mage YoungBloom appeared behind AngerHeart. Right away, she cast Greater Healing. A bright white light formed in her palms, then floated like a small silver ball into AngerHeart's chest.

AngerHeart leaped to his feet and crashed his shoulder into DeathBringer's shield. The great demon was knocked to his back, his shield split in two.

The demon threw his shattered shield aside and climbed to his feet. "Your allies cannot help you, fools," he said. Then DeathBringer cast a mighty burst of flames at YoungBloom. She fell to the grass, defeated.

Mark looked down to see YoungBloom's card burn and curl inward. In seconds, it became a pile of ashes.

DeathBringer bellowed, "I cannot be defeated!"

The boys cast every ally card they had. They sent in healers and thieves and rangers. They called warrior after warrior. They called great bears and dire wolves and even a phoenix. The demon god destroyed all of them, quickly and easily.

Finally, AngerHeart was alone on the field, face to face with DeathBringer.

There were no more allies or pet cards to play. Mark and Alex had tapped them all, using every ability they could. Dozens of small piles of ashes rested at their feet. Only AngerHeart's card remained.

DeathBringer stomped across the field toward the warrior. He swung his morning star at AngerHeart. The warrior blocked it with his armored glove, but DeathBringer slammed his other fiery fist into AngerHeart's visor, knocking the warrior to the ground.

The demon pushed down on AngerHeart's mailed chest with heavy, black greaves.

DeathBringer raised his weapon and swirled it over his head. "Now you die," he said. "And this mortal world becomes mine!"

## ~ Chapter 8: Stabbed in the Back ~

Mark knew he had to do something. He scanned DeathBringer's card with his eyes, desperately looking for some sort of clue.

Then he had an idea. Mark stood up, holding DeathBringer's card. "Not so fast!" he said. "I have one more weapon to cast."

"No weapon will save your warrior now, mortal," DeathBringer said through a laugh.

"Oh, yeah?" Mark said. "I cast Demon Dagger!" He tapped DeathBringer's card, summoning a green dagger that had a one-hundred-point attack power bonus against demons.

The magical weapon appeared in DeathBringer's hand. It was jagged and glowed with a demonic red energy.

DeathBringer laughed. "You fool!" he said. "Did you think my special weapon would help this weak human warrior? He cannot equip this dagger. Only I can!"

With that, the demon threw the dagger into the ground. It stuck into the ground only feet from Mark and Alex, making them leap back in fear.

The demon growled fiercely as he turned back to face AngerHeart.

DeathBringer raised his weapon over his head and prepared to bring it down on the unconscious warrior.

Mark smiled. *You're wrong, DeathBringer,* Mark thought. He reached down and grabbed the dagger by the hilt.

Mark felt its power flow through him, making him feel super-strong, fast, and confident. *I played your card,* Mark thought. *That means I, too, can use this dagger!* He ran toward the demon.

DeathBringer brought his weapon down with fearsome force. Just as the morning star was about to slam into AngerHeart's head, Mark dug the dagger deep into DeathBringer's armored back. The glowing dagger split the demon's armor like a pocket knife through marshmallow.

Mark's blow made the demon's morning star shift. It hit the ground just inches from AngerHeart's skull.

"No!" DeathBringer cried out.

Mark raised the dagger high over his head. He brought it down into the back of the demon's helm, lodging it into DeathBringer's skull.

DeathBringer screamed in pain. Silver light burst from the weapon, throwing Mark from the demon's back. He landed on the grass with a hard thud.

Alex hobbled over to him, and the boys watched as the sliver of light grew. Soon the demon was surrounded by a ball of silver light. Then it vanished — and so did DeathBringer.

Mark pulled out DeathBringer's card. It was blank, just a thin sheet of dull metal.

"He's gone," Mark whispered.

Tired, AngerHeart climbed to his feet. He walked toward the boys and placed his armored gloves on their shoulders. "You have done well," he said.

Mark and Alex smiled at each other. "The demon is defeated," AngerHeart said. His voice was tired and hoarse, and his armor was blackened and dented. "Your world is safe — for now."

"What about you?" Alex asked. "I still have your card." He held it up for AngerHeart to see.

AngerHeart smiled at Alex. "I have fought countless battles with you, Alex," AngerHeart said. "But I have grown tired of fighting. My time must come to an end now."

"What?" Alex cried. "You saved us! You can't just . . ."

"I can," AngerHeart said. His proud head was hung low, as if he were admitting defeat. "And I must. Besides, other, stronger warriors will take my place in the next expansion pack."

AngerHeart backed away from the two boys. "Rip the card in half," he pleaded. "And end my suffering."

Mark's shoulders sank. He could tell the warrior had made his decision. He looked over to Alex and his friend nodded. Reluctantly, Mark lifted AngerHeart's card and held it between his hands by the fingers. "Goodbye," Mark said. "And thank you."

Mark ripped the card in half . . . but nothing happened. Mark and Alex stared up at AngerHeart, confused.

Just then, lightning streaked across the sky, crackling over and over above the town of Ravens Pass. Thunder shook the ground. The air seemed to be electrified.

AngerHeart leaned in close to Mark. The foul stench of his breath invaded Mark's nostrils. AngerHeart's eyes grew red, glowing so devilishly that they seemed to dig into Mark's skull.

"No," AngerHeart said, grabbing Mark and Alex with his metal fists. "Thank *you* for helping me get rid of the competition."

**Case number:** 232960

**Date reported:** May 18

**Crime scene:** Ravens Pass High School football stadium

**Civilian witnesses:** Mark Gannon, age 14; Alex Reid, age 14

**Disturbance:** Mark Gannon and Alex Reid, eighth-graders at Ravens Pass Middle School, somehow managed to summon two ancient demons into our realm.

**Evidence:** The Ravens Pass football stadium was torn to shreds. Additionally, after some investigative research on the Epic Warriors trading card company, I discovered that the company's CEO had several ties to a local Ravens Pass cult that practices black magic.

**Suspect:** Tyler Wulfe, CEO of the Epic Warriors trading card company

CASE NOTES:

AFTER THEIR DUEL WITH A PAIR OF DEMONS, MARK AND ALEX APPROACHED TYLER WULFE TO TALK TO HIM ABOUT THE DANGERS OF HIS CARD GAME. INSTEAD, WULFE HAD THEM EXPELLED FROM SCHOOL AND CHARGED WITH VANDALISM OF THE FOOTBALL STADIUM. THAT'S WHEN MARK AND ALEX CAME TO ME FOR HELP.

I PAID TYLER WULFE A SURPRISE VISIT. AT FIRST, HE SAID HE DIDN'T HAVE TIME FOR SOME CRAZY DETECTIVE. BUT WHEN I SAID I HAD PROOF THAT HE WAS PRACTICING BLACK MAGIC, TYLER QUICKLY CHANGED HIS TUNE AND INVITED ME INTO HIS OFFICE. AS I ENTERED, HE HANDED ME WHAT HE SAID WAS HIS BUSINESS CARD. AS I EXAMINED IT, I SAW THAT IT WAS ACTUALLY A BLANK EPIC WARRIORS TRADING CARD. STARING AT THE CARD, I FELT A STRANGE PULL TOWARD IT. IT SEEMED TO BE CALLING TO ME. I'D SEEN THIS TYPE OF THING BEFORE — AN ENTRAPMENT SPELL IS EASY TO IDENTIFY, IF YOU KNOW WHAT TO LOOK FOR.

I FLIPPED THE CARD OVER JUST IN TIME. WRITHING AND SCREAMING, TYLER WAS SUCKED INTO THE TRADING CARD. THAT'S WHERE HE'LL STAY UNTIL I CAN CAPTURE THE OTHER CULT MEMBERS AND BRING THEM TO JUSTICE.

DEAR READER,

THEY ASKED ME TO WRITE ABOUT MYSELF. THE FIRST THING YOU NEED TO KNOW IS THAT JASON STRANGE IS NOT MY REAL NAME. IT'S A NAME I'VE TAKEN TO HIDE MY TRUE IDENTITY AND PROTECT THE PEOPLE I CARE ABOUT.

YOU WOULDN'T BELIEVE THE THINGS I'VE SEEN, WHAT I'VE WITNESSED. IF PEOPLE KNEW I WAS TELLING THESE STORIES, SHARING THEM WITH THE WORLD, THEY'D TRY TO GET ME TO STOP. BUT THESE STORIES NEED TO BE TOLD, AND I'M THE ONLY ONE WHO CAN TELL THEM.

I CAN'T TELL YOU MANY DETAILS ABOUT MY LIFE. I CAN TELL YOU I WAS BORN IN A SMALL TOWN AND LIVE IN ONE STILL. I CAN TELL YOU I WAS A POLICE DETECTIVE HERE FOR TWENTY-FIVE YEARS BEFORE I RETIRED. I CAN TELL YOU I'M STILL OUT THERE EVERY DAY AND THAT CRAZY THINGS ARE STILL HAPPENING.

I'LL LEAVE YOU WITH ONE QUESTION—IS ANY OF THIS TRUE?

JASON STRANGE
RAVENS PASS

## Glossary

**allies** (AL-eyez)—friends and supporters

**ally** (AL-eye)—a person that gives support to another

**decay** (di-KAY)—rot or break down

**destroy** (di-STROI)—to ruin something or someone completely

**faction** (FAK-shuhn)—a united group

**helm** (HELM)—a hard hat made of metal that protects a knight's head during battle

**hilt** (HILT)—the handle of a sword or dagger

**mace** (MAYSS)—a club-like weapon

**morning star** (MOR-ning STAR)—a medieval weapon made of a spiked metal ball that is connected to a shaft by a metal chain

**ruined** (ROO-ind)—destroyed something completely

**singed** (SINJD)—burned slightly

**smoldering** (SMOHL-dur-ing)—burning and smoking

**summon** (SUHM-uhn)—to call or request someone to come

**wicked** (WIK-id)—cruel or evil

# DISCUSSION QUESTIONS

1. What games do you like to play? Video games? Card games? Other types of games? Talk about your favorite games.

2. Which Epic Warrior was your favorite? DeathBringer? AngerHeart? YoungBloom? GraceBlood? Why?

3. What part of this book did you think was the scariest? Why?

1. Create your own Epic Warrior. What kind of armor, weapons, and magical abilities does your warrior have? Write about it, then draw a picture of your warrior.

2. Alex and Mark thought they could trust AngerHeart, but he ended up betraying them. Write about a time when your trust was broken.

3. What happens after this book ends? Write another chapter to this story.

Weird
THINGS
happen in
RAVENS
PASS.

JASON STRANGE

writes about them.

**for more**

# monsters
# GHOSTS
# secrets

## JASON STRANGE

# creatures

visit us at www.capstonepub.com

Find cool websites and more books
like this one at www.facthound.com.
Just type in the Book ID: 9781434232960